Baby Its Cold Outside

A CHRISTMAS NOVELLA

WHISKEY FALLS

BOOK ONE

KIMBERLY ANN

Independently Published

Cover design by: Pages & Pines

Edited by: Daley Author Services

Proofreading by: Romance Me With Books

Chapter One

There's Christmas magic in the air. I can feel it.

I can't contain my smile as I step out of my run down sedan, taking in the wintery scene before me. Snowflakes fall in large chunks, covering every surface of the pavement beneath my boots. The snow has been relentless for the last two days, covering everything in a thick blanket of white. You'd think we would be used to it, living in the middle of British Columbia where the snow is ruthless, but year after year everyone seems just as unprepared as the last. I'm usually the first one to roll my eyes and get on with my day, but it's especially bad today. My car slid a few times getting here, making me question if I made the right choice going through with this, but in the end, I was determined to make it, no matter what.

Most people wouldn't have made the same choice. They would have stayed home, safe in their houses.

But no, not me.

As I slam my car door, I see a small path has been left in the mountain of snow between the street and the sidewalk. I throw up a quick 'thank you' for this little piece of luck. I've made it here, barely, without incident. The last thing I want to

1

do is sink thigh-deep into the pile of dirty snow left by the plows.

Determined to get out of the cold as quickly as I can, I stomp my snow-covered boots on the cement, knocking off the thick layer of white that built up on my short walk. Placing my hand on the iron handle of the solid oak door, I pull back and am mildly surprised by its weight. It's so heavy, I wouldn't be surprised if it was the original door instead of the flimsy glass ones they make now. This place has been here for as long as I can remember, and now that I think about it, it hasn't changed much from the outside.

I let out a slight grunt as I pull as hard as I can with my glove-covered hand, hoping I don't slip and land on my ass in the snow behind me. That's all I'd need to start the night off.

While I wouldn't have chosen The Lucky Dog Pub as an ideal first date location, I have to admit from the outside it doesn't look too bad compared to some of the other places I've met dates from the same app. I've met guys at coffee shops, the diner, even the rodeo one time. The worst had to be a dingy bowling alley in the next town over. Thankfully, I had taken my car and met him there. I snuck out without even a 'goodbye' after I found out it was really just a night he'd planned with his friends and then got drunk and ignored me most of the night.

Even though I grew up in Whiskey Falls, I've never been into the bar scene, which is why I've never been to this one before. There's also been talk of it having a new owner—one not from our small town—which has sent the town into a gossiping frenzy.

Stepping further into the dimly lit bar, I embrace the warmth as I pull off my gloves and scarf, quickly adjusting to the change in temperature.

A long, dark-stained wooden bar runs the length of the wall across from me. Shelves of liquor of varying colours are lined up behind the countertop. Large booths line one wall, their red leather looking worn from years of use. There are high-top tables scattered throughout the room, circling a stage that is tucked away in the corner with a small dance floor in front. All empty.

What really captures my attention is the lone, scarcely decorated tree sitting in the corner by the stage; only a single silver strand of tinsel garland thrown haphazardly over the branches. Miniature twinkling lights hang above the bar while classic Christmas music plays softly through the speakers.

I make my way over to one of the high-top tables, my boots echoing through the empty space, making it even more apparent how alone I am. In a bar I don't know. Which apparently doesn't even have a bartender on duty tonight. Sure, Whiskey Falls is a safe town, but I've learned a woman can never be too careful. Why didn't I tell one of my brothers where I was going? Or Cara?

I shake my head as I drape my jacket over the back of the chair, hanging my purse on the corner. It's too late now. Now, I just have to hope for the best.

I pull out my phone, seeing that I'm ridiculously early. I did this on purpose, hoping to settle my nerves before my date showed up. Normally, I would do this with a glass of wine, but since there wasn't anyone around, I can only dwell on the thoughts rushing through my mind.

What if he doesn't show?

What if he's like all the other jerks I've been meeting lately?

What if he only wants to hook up? No meaningful conversation. No relationship that lasts longer than a night.

Meeting on a dating app was never how I thought I'd find a man, but with working so hard on my year-round Christmas ornament business, it leaves little time for me, let alone meeting anyone else. I only broke down and signed up for the app when my friend Cara made a profile for me. We spent a wine-fuelled night swiping left and right on everyone that crossed my screen.

That's where I found Mack. He's handsome, in a college frat-guy sort of way, and close to my age of twenty-five. We chatted over texts for a week before deciding to meet up for drinks. In fact, he was the one that suggested we meet on Christmas Eve. My favourite holiday. I convinced myself it was fate.

Now, as I sit alone in a bar with enough snow outside to shut down an entire city, I'm not so sure.

Is there even a bartender here?

As if on cue, the most handsome man that has ever roamed the Earth walks into the room carrying a large plastic tub that clinks of glass with every step he takes.

His short, dark brown hair is perfectly styled in a way that's meant to look naturally messy. A lock falls, briefly to the side, giving me the urge to rush over and swipe it off his face for him. His short, neatly trimmed beard matches his hair, the darkness a striking contrast to his intense ocean-blue eyes.

His step falters as he looks up and sees me, but he recovers quickly. I can't take my eyes off his arms as his muscles bulge in his blue plaid button-up, straining against the fabric as he lifts the tub onto the bar top. The cuffs have been rolled up to his elbows, showing his forearms with tattoos snaking their way up, disappearing into the fabric of his shirt. Arms have never really grabbed my attention before, but with him, I can't look away.

"Sorry, I didn't hear you come in." My eyes snap to his, breaking me from the trance his arms have over me. A shiver runs down my spine at his voice. It's deep and gravely, like taking a sip of strong whiskey over ice.

I'd give anything to listen to him read a romance audiobook.

"It's okay. I just got here." I barely recognize my voice with the unfiltered rasp of desire lacing through it.

Who am I?

I clear my throat, hoping to sound more in control than I really am. Sitting up straighter, I force myself to remember I'm here for a reason other than to ogle the bartender. "I'm waiting for someone."

He walks to my table, bringing his scent of sandalwood and leather with him. It takes every last drop of self-restraint I have, but I resist the urge to fist his shirt in my hands, close my eyes, and lean into him.

What is wrong with me? I've never had such an instinctual reaction to a person before. I'm not the type who wants to grab strangers and smell them.

"What can I get you while you wait?" My eyes dart to his, and once again I find myself lost in them.

Orgasms. Lots of orgasms.

I give my head a slight shake. "A glass of red wine, please."

He raises his eyebrow questioningly before giving me a quick nod and makes his way back to the bar. My eyes trail down to the way his light blue, well-worn jeans mold to his ass as he walks away. He has a hockey player's bubble butt that gives way to strong thighs, which are currently maxing out the give on the denim.

"What brings you out in this storm?" He rounds the counter and grabs an upside-down wineglass by the stem. He expertly flips it around to sit on top of the bar with one hand while grabbing the wine bottle with the other.

"I would hardly call this a snowstorm," I add, not taking my eyes off him. His large, calloused hands seem too large to be handling the breakable glass so delicately, like he could snap the stem with one finger if he chose to.

His gaze meets mine as he takes the cap off the wine bottle

and starts pouring. "Last I checked, there wasn't much left for the snow to cover."

I laugh. "It's not the snow that's the problem; it's more the people in the city that don't know how to handle it."

"Fair enough." He walks over to the table, placing a coaster in front of me and my glass on top. "You still didn't answer my question."

I look up into his blue eyes, and it feels as if all the air in my chest leaves my body. They are such a vivid blue, and mixed with his striking features, they literally take my breath away. I freeze, not wanting to tell him the real reason I'm in the pub. I don't want to admit that I'm here to meet another man. "A date."

"Ah. Hopefully, your boyfriend makes it with the *non-storm* out there." The smirk on his face is distracting, almost making me miss the use of the word '*boyfriend*.'

"Not my boyfriend. A first date, actually." I force the words out casually as I pick up the wineglass and take a sip.

"On Christmas Eve?" he scoffs.

"Yes. What's wrong with having a date on Christmas Eve?" I retort, placing my glass back down on the table as carefully as I can. I take a deep breath, attempting to steady myself for what I'm sure is going to be an interesting commentary on dating during the holidays. But it's not only that. There's something about speaking with this incredibly gorgeous man that makes me nervous. I don't know why; it's not like I'm here on a date with him.

"Nothing." He walks back toward the bar, clearly meaning anything but '*nothing*.'

I look down at my phone, seeing that Mack is now five minutes late. Time flew by, talking to this blue-eyed cynic. I sigh, placing it back down on the table, face down.

I hate it when people are late. Mack's looking like all the other 'men' I've met on this app.

Grabbing my glass of wine, I follow the sexy bartender

back to the bar, where he's currently unloading the clean dishes from the tub he had just carried in. "Okay, tell me. What's wrong with a first date on Christmas Eve?"

He pauses while putting a glass on the shelf to look at me. "It's setting yourself up for failure. It's like some sort of big romantic gesture meant to show that it was 'meant to be,' when, in reality, it's too much pressure. Like a first date on New Year's Eve or Valentine's Day. There's no way that can go well."

Shit, isn't that exactly what I'm doing?

"Well, aren't you Mr. Romantic?" I ask dryly with a sarcastic smile. "I bet you have all the ladies lining up to be around you during the holidays."

"What makes you think I want anyone around for the holidays?" he asks coldly, grabbing another glass.

I turn my back on him, surveying the decorations around the bar. "For someone who doesn't, you sure—decorated. You could use some help, though."

"Those are only there because the regulars complained. I wasn't going to put anything up. This is my compromise." His voice is flat when he answers.

I turn, levelling a glare at him. "You're just a regular old Grinch, aren't you?"

"If you say so," he scoffs.

I return to my table, checking my phone one more time, hoping there's something telling me Mack is still on his way. I'm saddened to see there is only my lock screen showing a picture of me and my brothers smiling on the beach looking back at me. I sigh and drop my shoulders as I glance out the bar's window, watching the snow come down even harder than before.

What am I even doing here? Is he even going to show?

I should have listened to my brothers and just deleted the dating app after the first couple of horrible dates. I'm not even sure why I decided I needed to have a boyfriend, anyway. I've been happy on my own—mostly. Now that I think of it, it's only when I get closer to the holidays that I get lonely. It's when I notice the couples doing couple-things that I realize I want that. When I see them walking hand-in-hand through the town's Christmas festival or ice skating at the rink. When I see my friends and their significant others dressed in matching Christmas sweaters and kissing under the mistletoe. That's when I notice I want that. The romance. The companionship. That's what I'm missing out on.

Glancing over my shoulder, I look at the blue-eyed hottie as he glances away from my ass; caught in the act.

Maybe I don't need to find Mr. Right. Maybe Mr. Right Now isn't such a bad idea. After all, I have Christmas music, decent wine, and a handsome bartender, even if he belongs on Mount Crumpit with a dog at his side.

Chapter Two

BRETT

W ell, this is unexpected.

I was just about to shut everything down for the night, seeing how there hasn't been another soul in the bar all day. It takes a lot to keep the regulars away, especially during the holidays, but I guess the damn near blizzard outside finally did it. The only reason I even opened was because I live in the apartment upstairs and I had nothing better to do. I wanted to catch up on paperwork and some things I'd let slide during the pre-Christmas rush, leaving the door open in case someone needed a drink and a place to warm up.

What I didn't expect was this beautiful blonde to appear in my bar, acting as if Whiskey Falls wasn't experiencing the worst snowstorm it has seen in decades.

She isn't like the other women that come in here. Her curly blonde hair and big blue eyes make her look too innocent to be in a place like The Lucky Dog. While not the unruliest establishment I've been in, it's not a place where strikingly beautiful women choose to spend their evenings, especially on Christmas Eve.

As she walks up to the bar, I can't help but gaze at her

sweater, which is embroidered with Christmas lights along the neckline complimented by tiny jingle bell earrings hanging from her ears. It looks like something my mom would have worn while I was growing up. Somehow, this angel makes it look less vintage and more adorable as it fits perfectly to her hot body. What doesn't bring back childhood holiday memories is the black pants that fit her like a glove, molding to her curves like they were made just for her.

Images flash through my mind of placing my hands on that gorgeous ass, curling my hands into the generous globes, picking her up, and thrusting her against a wall while she wraps her legs around me.

I shake my head, clearing those thoughts from my mind. She's here to meet a date. Another man. Not here to have me think lewd thoughts about her. It's not her fault that it's been so long since I've been with a woman that I'm now picturing my customers with their hair wrapped around my fist and my body between their thighs. But it's not just any customer. It's only her. I don't even know her name and yet she's put me on edge like no other woman has in a very long time.

I reach down and pull at my jeans, which have become uncomfortably tight. I'm thankful for the bar that's currently blocking her view of just how badly I need to get laid.

"I don't think your date is going to make it. It's getting really bad out there." I busy myself by putting the last of the clean glasses on the shelf, hating the frown that crosses her face at my words.

"I'll give him a couple more minutes. You never know." Her eyes double in size as she looks up at me. "You don't think anything happened to him, do you?"

"I'm sure he's fine. Probably just got stuck or didn't make it out."

"Maybe," she answers, her voice low as she looks down at the screen in her hand.

The pain in her voice is like a stab to my heart. Why is this stranger affecting me so much?

"Or maybe I should just go," she says sadly, turning from me before pulling out a couple of bills and placing them on the table. "I'm sorry to waste your time. Merry Christmas."

"Wait." I round the bar, closing the distance between us in just a few steps. Without thinking, I grab her hand, stopping her from lifting her jacket off the chair. I'm not prepared for the electricity that tears through my arm where we touch, shooting straight to my groin. I've never had a reaction like this from someone before, especially from someone I just met. The excitement. The rush. I don't want to let her go. I know I need to do anything I can to make her stay. "Have another drink. I can't let you go out there when it's snowing so fiercely."

Now that I'm standing closer to her, I can't help but notice how much shorter she is than me. Even with her high heels, she only comes to the middle of my chest. Perfect for reaching down and throwing over my shoulder.

My body stills. Where the fuck did that come from? I've never thrown a woman over my shoulder in my life. There's something about this wide-eyed blonde that has me thinking things I shouldn't.

She looks back out the window without taking her hand from mine. I take it as a small win, even if she's still contemplating leaving.

"It's fine. I've got an all-wheel drive."

I give her hand a squeeze, drawing her attention from the window back to me. "Please. I don't want anything to happen to you."

"You don't even know me. Why are you so worried about me?" Her voice is barely above a whisper as her blue eyes pierce into mine.

"I don't know. There's something about you…"

What the fuck is wrong with me?

"I'm Brett Jansen, the owner of The Lucky Dog. Yes, you pinned me properly—I'm not a Christmas fan, but something tells me this might be my best one yet."

A beautiful smile crosses her face. "Hi, Brett. I'm Krissy Winters. I am a lover of all things Christmas. So much so that I make handmade Christmas ornaments year-round."

Without thinking, I rub the inside of her wrist with my thumb. "Year-round, huh? There are people buying Christmas ornaments in the summer?"

Her eyes open wide as she rocks to the balls of her feet, excitement written all over her face. "There sure are! People want to buy them on special occasions, to remember holidays, or as a joke gift. Some of my busiest times are in the summer."

"Why don't I get you that second drink, and you can tell me all about it?" I lead her back to the bar and motion for her to sit at a stool before taking my place behind the counter and grabbing her another glass.

She gives me a sly smile as she settles into her seat. "Only if you get one for yourself, too."

"I think I can do that," I chuckle.

I pour another glass of wine and slide it in front of her before grabbing a whiskey on the rocks for myself. Taking a seat on a stool beside her, I raise my glass and clink it with hers as she does the same.

"So, what kind of ornaments are they?" I ask, taking a sip of my whiskey.

"Oh, all sorts!" Krissy's eyes lit up with excitement. "Anything you can think of, I can make. Popular ones are for families, pets, weddings, baby's first Christmas, that sort of thing. What I love the most is when I get unique requests."

"How unique can ornaments be? Isn't it all Christmas trees and reindeer?" I ask, leaning forward. I swear she smells like gingerbread and fresh snow, even though I don't know how that's possible.

"There's so much more than just trees and reindeer! My

favourite request is probably an ornament in the shape of a toilet that said, 'This year belongs in the shitter.'"

I laugh loudly, unable to contain my amusement. "You've got to be kidding me. Someone ordered that?"

"Yup!" Krissy chuckled. "That's one reason I love what I do. It's never boring."

I take a sip of whiskey, my eyes drawn to the smile on her lips as she takes a sip of her wine. Her eyes glimmer in the low light of the bar, reminding me of the lights Archer made me hang last week. He said the bar was 'too depressing' for people who were already depressed. I don't know what some dollar store lights are going to do for those struggling, but it was worth a shot for my patrons.

They were worth every penny if it means her eyes glimmer like that all night.

"So, your turn. Why own a bar?" She tilts her head as she asks.

"No real story there. I saw it as a good business decision. There's always someone looking for a drink in Whiskey Falls, and this place came up for sale at the right time."

"That makes sense, especially when the rodeo is in town." She eyes me carefully as she traces the rim of her wineglass with her finger. Her nails are painted a deep red with a white snowflake design.

She wasn't kidding when she said she loves Christmas.

I notice the colour of her nails also matches her lipstick. In that moment, I can't help but think of how her hand and mouth would look wrapped around my cock, kneeling in front of me, looking up at me with those big blue eyes of hers. That image alone is enough to get me into the Christmas spirit.

"So, I guess my next question is, why are you such a grinch?" she asks, breaking me from my holiday-induced vision.

"Excuse me? I'm not a grinch," I scoff as I lean back on my stool.

"So why the sad decorations, then?" She lets her gaze travel over my shoulder.

I turn, looking to see it as she did. I originally thought I had done a pretty good job decorating, given my lack of supplies and desire to decorate at all. Christmas is never one of the top holidays I consider celebrating. I'm usually working or alone at this time of the year and I would rather just forget the entire month of December, if I were completely honest. The only reason I entertained the regulars was because happy customers mean more sales.

"They aren't sad. I hung lights. There's a tree. I even changed the music." I can't help the defensiveness in my tone as I turn back to her. I wasn't about to run all over town buying expensive decorations when they would only sit in a box eleven months out of the year.

"Please. A five-year-old could do better," Krissy scoffs as she stands up, placing her hands on her hips. "Where's your storage room? You must have more decorations than this."

"You can't be serious." I take another look at her festive sweater and realize my mistake. "Oh shit, you are serious."

She reaches over and tugs at my arm, causing the same electric charge from before to shoot through my body and straight to my cock.

"Come on, you must have something else somewhere. Where are you hiding them?" she asks with a coy smile.

"Shouldn't you be focusing on your date? He might be here any minute." I know I'm being an ass for bringing it up, but it's me that needs the reminder. She's not here for me. She's here to meet another man.

"You're probably right," she sighs, walking back to the table and picking up her phone, growling at the screen. "Looks like he's not coming, anyway."

Walking back to me, she faces her phone so I can see her screen.

MACK

Sorry. No go tonight. Fucking snow. Maybe next time.

Douchebag. Who calls off a date with a text like that?

"I'm sorry your date didn't work out as planned." I mean what I say—mostly. While I'm not happy that asshole left her waiting for him, I'm happy it means she's in my bar tonight.

At first, she shrugs with a sad look on her face before placing her phone on the bar top. A moment later, however, her face breaks out into a wide smile as she bounces on the spot and claps her hands. "Oooh, that means I can help you decorate!"

Well, fuck.

Chapter Three

KRISSY

I don't know why I'm so invested in making The Lucky Dog look more festive, but I am. What I should do is pack up my things and go home before the snow gets too bad to drive. I should thank Brett and let him get on with his Christmas Eve instead of hanging decorations that won't be seen by anyone but the two of us.

But I don't.

Am I being pushy? Yes, but I'm determined to make it as Christmas-y as it can be. Everyone deserves a little holiday spirit. Even the grumpiest of the grumps, like Brett.

Plus, Mack isn't coming. It's snowing like a snow globe outside, and it's Christmas Eve. I might as well make it fun.

With a sigh, Brett throws back the rest of his whiskey and stands. He doesn't look at me as he lengthens his spine to his full, magnificent height, and walks down the darkened hallway I saw him come from earlier. Heaven help me, I can't help but follow him.

"Are you sure you want to do this? I mean, it's just us here, and I'm closed tomorrow. No one else is going to see this." Brett lowers his voice as he stops in front of the first door and turns to me.

"Yes, even if it's just for us." I can't stop the way my voice takes on a breathy hilt or the way my body leans into him, seeking him out. It takes every ounce of will in my body not to reach out and place my palm on his chest; feel the beat of his heart. Hope it's racing just as fast as mine.

He holds my gaze for a moment, letting my words float in the air between us. His intense blue eyes hold mine, making my breath catch.

He's so handsome. All thoughts I had about Mack are gone as I look into Brett's ocean blue eyes.

With a brief nod, he turns and opens the door, breaking my trance. Flicking on the lights, he makes a grand sweeping motion with his hand for me to enter the room.

I step past him, looking over my shoulder to make sure he isn't going to lock me in the room or do something equally baffling. He is a stranger, after all. Even if he is a sexy, intense, grumpy stranger.

Seeing he isn't going to hold me captive, I let myself survey the room, taking in the haphazardly labelled boxes that are stacked on the shelves that line the walls. A free-standing shelf, packed with even more boxes, sits in the middle of the room, creating two aisles.

"Alright, I don't know what's in here. The previous owner left everything a mess. I tried to organize it the best I could when I bought this place. I know there was a box or two more, but I don't know where they are. I just pulled out what I wanted to use."

Taking a step forward, I run my fingertips along the sides of the boxes, making my way down the aisle closest to me. A faint layer of dust coats my fingers as I gingerly stroke them. I resist the urge to wipe them off on my pants. Instead, I keep going, smiling as I gaze at the messy handwriting adorned on each cardboard box.

Napkins, glasses, straws.

They must be in here somewhere.

17

"Are you just going to stand there, or are you going to help me?" I turn to face Brett, placing my hands on my hips. The coarse wool fabric of my sweater is a welcome change from the gritty dust.

I take in the way he leans against the doorframe, arms crossed over his broad chest, one ankle crossed over the other. The white t-shirt under his blue plaid button up is straining against his muscles.

He's so damn sexy.

He chuckles as he pushes himself up. "Of course."

In any other scenario, I wouldn't be here talking with him. I'd be at home reading a book or at the store working on an ornament. This handsome lumberjack of a bar owner would scowl at the men in his bar or be fighting off the women throwing themselves at him.

Something occurs to me, which I should have thought about before. What if he has a woman back home? Why would I just assume this drop dead gorgeous man is single?

My eyes shoot to his hands, which are currently folded into his arms across his chest. I would have noticed a ring on his finger before, right?

I can't let myself go there. Then again, I'm not one to have the best judgement with men lately. It would be my luck that the only guy that's held my interest for longer than five seconds would be married or attached.

There's something about him. Something that's so captivating. More than he's classically handsome and could be on the cover of a magazine—or romance novel—just as much as he could own a bar. It's something else about Brett that I just can't put my finger on, but it's unlike anything I've ever felt before.

I pull my attention away from the sexy Christmas-hater with the devastating smirk, which is a feat that should put me at the top of Santa's nice list. For life. But I can't let him distract me. I have an important task at hand.

Making my way down the aisles, I rummage through boxes and scan the hastily written labels until I come across 'Xmas Shit' high on the top shelf.

"Found it!" I reach up, trying to grab the bottom of the box to slide it toward me. Even with my heeled boots, I'm still too short to reach it.

Before I know it, Brett's body presses against me, arms reaching up over mine. His presence is so overwhelming I need to close my eyes to take it all in. The heat of his body at my back engulfs me, contrasting against the cold of the metal shelves pressed against my chest. His scent, his own unique blend, wraps around me; I want to know what it feels like to have him put his big, tattooed arms around me and pull me close to him. I want to know what it would be like to have a man like him make me his.

"Here, let me. You look like you're going to hurt yourself."

The moment is lost when he slides the box above my head and turns, placing it at his feet. My body sags at the loss of his touch; I don't dare to move, not sure what to do next when he takes a step forward, rewarding me once against with his touch. He places his hands on my shoulders and I lean back into him, my body resting against his, my head on his chest. I love that I'm so much shorter than him. That his body is so big, like he could wrap me up and protect me without even trying.

He lets out a deep sigh, letting the smoky scent of whiskey on his breath brush my cheek. He takes a moment, squeezing my shoulders, holding me against his body before running his hands down my arms, leaving a wake of goosebumps on my skin. Even with my sweater between us, I can feel the heat from him as if he were touching my bare skin.

Glancing down, I see the lack of a ring on his left hand and I send up another silent thank you. I would hope a man attached to someone else wouldn't be doing this with me, but my recent foray into dating would suggest that not all men are what I think they should be.

"There's another box." His voice in my ear is nothing more than a rumble that leads to a shiver that runs down my spine. My body feels like it's both on fire and on pins and needles, just with his voice in my ear.

"Okay," I croak, immediately bringing my hand up to my throat, trying to calm the nerves rising through my body.

"I need you to move aside," he says with a slight chuckle, but doesn't move to let me pass.

I smile, letting my head tilt, looking up into his deep blue eyes. "Okay."

He chuckles again and gives my arms a light squeeze, dropping his head where my shoulder meets my neck. I want to reach up and run my hands through his hair. I want to pull him closer to me. I want his arm to sneak around my waist and pull me against him.

I want so many things that I have no right to have.

A light brush against my exposed skin makes me stifle a moan. I don't know if it's the scrape of his neatly trimmed beard or a soft kiss, but whichever it is makes me sigh and sink further into him. I bite my lip and press my legs together, hoping it's not so obvious that everything this man does turns me on. Maybe it's just been too long since I've been with someone, but I've also never had anyone cause me to have such a physical reaction before.

Without warning, he takes a step back, almost causing me to lose my footing. A shiver runs up my spine at the sudden loss of heat and the effect he has on me.

Taking a step to the side, I bite back my pout and watch as he reaches up with his thick, sexy arms and grabs the other box labelled 'More Xmas Shit' in black marker. He places it on top of the other box, scanning the rest of the shelf. "I think that's it."

"Great." I look down, avoiding his glare. Awareness

prickles my skin. We're alone together, in this tiny room, snowed in at the bar. Just the two of us.

Did I imagine the fire that passed between us? Am I the only one that feels it? My mind replays every sigh, every touch, praying that I didn't just make a fool out of myself in front of Brett.

He clears his throat, drawing my attention back to him, and holds a box out to me. "Here. This one's light."

I take it from him in a daze as he turns and bends to pick up the other box at his feet.

Damn, that ass is going to get me into trouble.

I follow him out of the storage room, shutting off the light, and closing the door behind me. I take a deep breath, trying to steady my racing heart as I walk back into the bar.

Placing the box on a stool, I open the dusty flap and peer inside. "Alright, let's see what we've got here."

I sort through silver garlands, a star tree topper, a strand of lights with some broken bulbs, and a few knick-knack ornaments. I sigh and slump my shoulders. "Well, this isn't what I was hoping for."

Brett opened his box, peering inside with a frown. "I don't think you're going to like this box any better."

Walking over to him, I look, not bothering to hide the squeal that comes out of my mouth as I rummage through the box, becoming more and more excited at what I find. "Jackpot!"

The first thing I grab is a Santa hat. Placing it on my head, I reach back into the box and grab an identical one. I take a step toward Brett with my hands reaching to his perfectly messy-styled hair. He ducks at the last moment, leaving me reaching with the hat for an empty space.

"No way. I don't think so," he says, raising an eyebrow at me.

I cross my arms over my chest while clutching the hat, smirking at the way his gaze drifts down to my breasts. They may be hidden by my Christmas sweater, but it doesn't stop him from glancing at how they are being pushed up by my arms.

"What were you saying about not being a grinch?" I raise my eyebrow back at him in a silent challenge.

"I can tolerate Christmas without wearing *that*." He nods his chin at the red and white felt in my hand, a look of disgust on his face.

"It's just a hat, Brett. It's not going to hurt you." I chuckle as I take a step toward him.

He narrows his eyes at the offending fabric, taking a step back for every one I take forward. "Maybe not physically."

"You're impossible, Brett Jensen." I drop my hand with a laugh, throwing the hat back into the box.

"You're beautiful, Krissy Winters." I don't think I'm meant to hear the soft words that come from behind me, but I do. I close my eyes and smile, bracing my hands on the box in front of me.

I'm elated to know I didn't make up what happened in the storage room, and can only hope this means that he feels the same way about me as I do for him.

It also means there is hope I'll get him into the Christmas spirit.

Chapter Four

BRETT

I can't help myself as I watch Krissy move around my bar, hanging decorations like she owns the place. I should help, or at least trail behind and carry a box for her, but I'm sitting back at the high-top table, drinking whiskey, and enjoying the view.

As much as I don't want to, I'm feeling what I assume she means by the 'Christmas spirit.' My heart feels lighter and my body relaxes into my chair. I smile as she hangs the cheap lights and sways her hips to the carols playing through the speakers, drawing my attention to her glorious ass.

I let my eyes roam over her lithe body as she reaches up to place the star on the fake tree I have on the stage. She looks over her shoulder at me with a smile that would knock me off my feet if I weren't already sitting down.

"What do you think? Much better, right?"

I don't want to admit how sexy I find that stupid Santa hat on her head or the sweater that looks like it belongs in the nineties, but I do.

It's been so long since I've been with a woman. So long since one has even held my attention. Yet here I am, unable to take my eyes off this perky, Christmas-loving blonde.

Taking another slow sip of my whiskey, I let the smooth liquid burn down my throat as I watch her fuss with the garland on the tree. My eyes roam her body as I throw back what's left in my glass before placing it on the tabletop, not taking my eyes off of her. Closing the distance between us, I place my hands on her hips and pull her close until her back is flush with my chest.

She's so soft. So small.

I don't miss the gasp that escapes her lips. The urge to throw her over my shoulder and bring her upstairs to my apartment is almost too much. The desire to go full caveman on her wars with my need to hold her. Protect her.

Protect her from what? I don't know. Me, perhaps. I just know that I never want to let this beauty go now that I have her in my bar.

And to think, some douchebag passed up the opportunity to be with her.

Fucker. His loss is my gain.

I lean down until my mouth is at her ear. Her body shivers in my arms. "Are you sure your date isn't coming?"

"Yes." Her breath hitches when she answers.

"Are you upset by that?"

She tilts her head and looks over her shoulder at me. Her eyes find mine as she breathes, "No."

"Good." That's all I need to know as I cup her cheek and crash my lips down to hers. She turns her body in my arms to face me. Without breaking our kiss, she wraps her arms around my neck, drawing me in closer.

My free hand finds its way around her waist, pressing her as close to me as she can get.

She's just as soft as I imagine. Just as sweet. She tastes like wine and sugar cookies. An intoxicating combination, but one that suits her so well. I know from just one kiss I'm going to be addicted to her.

My hand slips from her cheek into her hair, gripping her

hard enough to hold her in place. Her hands slide from my neck to my chest, clutching my shirt, telling me she wants this just as much as I do, which only turns me on more.

I need to stop this before we go too far here in the middle of my bar. Not that I don't want to. I would give anything to fuck her on the countertop or place her on the table of a booth and devour her like the Christmas feast she is. But she deserves more than that. When we have our first time, it won't be a quick fuck against the closest table. It'll be special, even if whatever this is between us doesn't last past tonight.

Leaning my body back from hers, I'm rewarded with a slight whimper as her eyes flutter open.

"Dance with me," I whisper.

"What?" Her head snaps back, looking into my eyes.

"I said, dance with me," I repeat, this time more firmly.

As if the universe wants to give her a slight nudge, Michael Buble's crooning mixed with Idina Menzel's soulful voice begins as they sing 'Baby, It's Cold Outside.'

Krissy nods, and I can't control the genuine smile that crosses my face. I'm not one to dance—ever—but there's something about her that makes me want to do just that. She makes me want to do a lot of things I wouldn't normally do.

She also makes me feel things I haven't felt in a very long time, and I don't know what to do about it.

Taking her hand, I lead her over to the makeshift dance floor. It's really just an open area I've created with the tables pushed back into an arc around the stage. Pulling her into my arms, I close my eyes as I sway. My heart grows as her head rests on my chest and her hand traces up to my shoulder, her fingers playing with the short hairs at the back of my head. I take in every moment, every touch, even though I know I will never forget a second of it.

I don't even try to stop myself as my hand moves up and down the small of her back, drawing her closer and closer until there is no space left between us. We don't say anything as we move, and it's not lost on me just how comfortable the silence is between us. Every other woman I've ever been with has wanted to fill the silence with mindless talk that usually drove me mad, but not Krissy. She seems just as content with the silence, enjoying the magic of the moment.

Right now, I can recognize there's Christmas magic at work, and it's unlike anything I've ever experienced before. The immediate connection beyond just our sexual attraction, the uncanny familiarity that we've taken to each other. I don't believe in fate, but it's as if there are other forces at work that brought us together, and on Christmas Eve of all days.

"The snow is getting really bad out there," Krissy says quietly, drawing me from my thoughts.

I spin us and look out the window. Kissing her softly on the head, I take her hand and lead her to the front, peering out the frost-covered windows. "Yeah, I wouldn't recommend driving." I turn to her. "Why don't you stay here?"

"Oh, I can't do that. I'm sure you don't want some random person staying with you over Christmas." Her voice is low as she looks past me out the window.

"You aren't some random person, and I certainly can't let you go out there." I give her a stern look before turning my attention back to the snow. "Which one is your car?"

She takes a step, raising a finger on her free hand to point at a snow mound facing the bar doors. "Uh, that one."

I chuckle. "Yeah, I don't think we'll be able to dig you out. The roads are dangerous, anyway." I turn to her, cupping her cheek. "Do you want to leave? If you don't feel comfortable, I'll make it work. I'll drive you home in my truck and I'll bring you your car tomorrow."

Krissy shakes her head, letting her soft waves bounce around her face. "No, it's not that."

"Then stay." I've never felt this vulnerable with a woman before, nor have I ever cared if one stayed or left for a very long time. I don't play the hook up game too much anymore, but when I did, it was more of a distraction than anything else. With Krissy, my body aches at the thought of her leaving. A feeling that is completely new to me. "I have an apartment above the bar. It's not much, but it's better than sitting on the stools all night."

"But we just decorated," she says with the most adorable pout, looking at the lone tree in the corner of the room.

"We can bring the tree upstairs." I cup her cheek, bringing her attention back to me. "I don't have hot chocolate or anything festive, but I have coffee, and we can bring up the bottle of wine. What do you say?"

"This is crazy." Her breathy tone immediately makes me think of how she would sound in bed. The moans she would make as I slide into her. Would she scream my name as she comes?

Suddenly, I'm very thankful for my lone apartment without neighbours.

"It is, but you wanted Christmas magic."

"That's true." She looks at me with an expression I can't quite decipher. It's somewhere between confusion and wonder before a coy smile crosses her face.

"Do you think Santa will still be able to find me? I wouldn't want to miss the excitement of finding out if I was on the naughty or nice list this year." She looks up at me with those crystal blue eyes as she walks her fingers up my chest. Her intimate touch makes my blood rush south. I can't think around her. Not past kissing her. Running my hands through her hair. Getting her upstairs so I can worship every inch of her body.

"Oh, there's no doubt that he will. Just like there's no doubt you'll be on the nice list." I drop my head, running my nose along the column over her neck, taking in the hitch in her breath and the shiver that runs through her body. "But I have a feeling you could be very, very naughty if you want to."

"Well, if *you're* on the nice list, maybe you'll find out," she says as she plays with the buttons on my shirt.

"Hmm, that one may be a bit harder. Let me lock up, and we'll move this Christmas party upstairs." I give her a quick kiss before making my way back to the bar to close up for the night.

It was purely by chance I had opened the bar at all tonight with the way it had been snowing, but luck, or Christmas magic, was on my side for bringing this angel into my life.

Chapter Five

KRISSY

W hat have I gotten myself into?

When I first set foot in The Lucky Dog Pub earlier that night, I thought I would meet Mack, have a few drinks, and get to know someone I had only hoped wasn't like all the other men I'd met on the dating app.

Boy, was I wrong.

Instead, I end up snowed in with the most gorgeous man I've ever seen, bullied him into decorating his bar, and am now following him up to his apartment.

This isn't me. I don't go home with men I don't know. Except, I don't really have a choice tonight.

And I was technically already at his home.

Brett was right, it would be next to impossible to dig my car out the way it's been snowing, and even the short drive home would be more dangerous than I would care to take on tonight.

It's nothing. Just because I'm going up to his apartment doesn't mean anything is going to *happen*. So then why is each step I take mixed with a bundle of excitement and nerves? We're adults. Adults can just talk. In the light of the

Christmas tree. After the most breathtaking, press-my-legs-together kiss I've ever had in my life.

There's no pressure or expectation from Brett. I know with every fibre in my being I'm safe with him. Judging by the events of the night, I'm a hell of a lot better snowed in with Brett than I would have been with Mack.

Fucking Mack.

Mack, who didn't even have the courtesy to tell me he wasn't going until he was already late. I should have known. Any guy that has more pictures of his truck and lakes than of him on his dating profile probably wasn't looking for more than a hookup.

Why do I keep picking these guys?

Then there was Brett, with his perfect denim-covered ass in front of me as he effortlessly carries the tree up with him. I can't help but be thankful there weren't any ornaments on it. If there had been, it certainly wouldn't have survived the trip. Artificial branches scrape along the narrow staircase, silver garland falls off and trails behind him. I had to sidestep it a few times, or I was sure I would have stepped on it and caused us both to trip. I *don't* need my clumsy tendencies to come out. Not in front of Brett. Not now. Not ever.

Clutching the bottle of wine and my purse to my chest, I stop briefly as Brett opens the door at the top of the staircase, barely slowing down or shifting the tree as he does.

"Please, come in." He strides to the corner of the apartment, setting the tree down by the window.

I follow, closing the door behind me, and taking the opportunity to survey the room. White walls stand empty, only a couch and a TV in the living room. A small kitchen in the corner with barely enough room for a sink and oven. The countertops are bare except for a loaf of bread in the corner. "Did you just move in?"

"Maybe about six months ago?" He answered, turning to me. "Is it that obvious?"

"You haven't decorated much." I can't help but chuckle as he places his hands on his hips and looks around.

"Yeah, I guess I never thought about it."

A wave of sadness hits me. Not only does he not have someone to decorate for the holidays with, but he doesn't even have anyone to make his apartment a home. No pictures or art hang on the walls. No sentimental knick-knacks. Nothing.

"Well, maybe you can start." I smile as I walk toward him, placing the wine and my purse on the couch. "I never asked you before, but I'm going to assume you aren't from Whiskey Falls."

He nods. "I'm from Logan Creek, but I move anywhere there's a job. That's how I ended up here."

"Logan Creek is beautiful. I'm surprised you wanted to leave." I take another step toward him, closing the distance between us.

"Logan Creek's smaller than Whiskey Falls. Not too many jobs for a drifter like me." He takes a step toward me, wrapping me in a scent of leather.

"Is that what you are? A drifter?" I look up at him, placing my hand on his chest. He responds by cupping my cheek, stroking my skin with his thumb. I can't help but close my eyes and take in the feel of him. I brand it to my memory, not knowing if we'll have anything past tonight. If he really is a drifter, he won't be staying for long, regardless of him owning the bar. Whiskey Falls has seen its fair share of people setting up shop for the rodeo season and leaving town once it is over. Maybe it's because of that, I need to make sure I remember every moment from tonight.

"I was." His voice is smooth and smoky as he speaks. I let it surround me. Give me hope.

"And now?" My eyes open, finding his.

"I don't know. I'm thinking Whiskey Falls is pretty special. There might be something to keep me around."

31

"Oh, yeah? And what might that be?" I ask, a smile growing as I look up at him.

"A pint-sized Christmas-loving elf. She seemed to waltz into my bar tonight and make me rethink some things." Brett wraps his arms around me, pulling me flush to him.

"Hmm, a Christmas elf, you say?" I tilt my head and go up on my tiptoes, wrapping my arms around his neck.

"Yeah. She's a little bossy, but really cute, so I'm willing to overlook some things." That smile he gives me melts my heart. In the glow of the Christmas tree in the corner, he looks like the leading man of a romantic holiday movie, ready to sweep me off my feet.

"Maybe she brought a little Christmas magic with her? Turning the bah-humbug into a big old elf."

"I wouldn't go that far," he chuckles. "But I might be warming up to the idea."

His hand spreads across my back, causing heat to course through my body. I press my thighs together to relieve some tension, but it doesn't help.

He pulls me even closer to him as he lowers his head and captures my mouth in a kiss. I can't stop my fingers from going in his hair, playing with the short strands as his tongue runs along my lips. Just like I can't stop myself from opening for him, deepening the kiss like my life depends on it.

I just met this man. I came to his bar to meet someone else.

Is this crazy? Yes.

Is this completely out of character for me? Also, yes.

Am I going to stop? Hell, no.

Without breaking our connection, Brett backs us up to the couch, taking a seat and pulling me onto his lap. Straddling him, I lower myself down, feeling just how much he wants this.

"We don't have to go any farther than this if you don't want to," he says, running his fingers through my hair. His eyes are full of desire as he looks up at me, making me melt.

"Just tell me what you want, my little elf. Anything you want, it's yours."

The desire laced through his words set my body on fire. I don't know what I did to deserve a night like this, But I'm going to take it and enjoy every second.

"You." I lace my hands at the base of his neck, rubbing my core along his hard, denim-covered length. "I want you."

"Thank fuck," he breathes, kissing my neck.

"Can I share a secret with you?" Butterflies fly around my stomach at a nauseating speed. I don't know what makes me want to confess this to him, as all my other boyfriends have balked at the idea and called me weird, but I feel the need to share this with Brett. I feel safe with him; like no matter what I tell him, he won't laugh or make fun of me.

Like he cares.

"You can tell me anything, babe." He pulls back, brushing my hair off my face.

"I've—uh—always wanted to make love by the light of the Christmas tree." I look down at our laps, afraid to see the judgement in his eyes. Afraid of seeing the same look I'm used to seeing. At least he's not laughing.

He places his knuckle under my chin, tipping my head until my eyes meet his. "Why do you look ashamed about that?"

"Other guys haven't been so—understanding." I take a deep breath, not able to control how fast the words fly out of my mouth. "There's just something so beautiful about the twinkling lights and the comforting feeling of the Christmas glow. I don't know. It's stupid." I try to look away, but he won't let me. He holds my chin, making me stay put.

"It's not stupid. I think it suits you, and if it's what you want, it's what you're going to get." With a quick kiss on my lips, he shifts and places me on the couch before standing, walking down the short hallway next to the kitchen.

I don't have time to wonder what he's doing. A moment

later, he reappears with a comforter and pillows, giving me a wink as he lays them all out in front of the tree. He pulls his phone out of his pocket and taps his screen a few times before Bing Crosby's crooning voice fills the apartment, singing about dreaming of a white Christmas.

How fitting.

He grabs the remote and turns on the TV, flipping through the channels until he brings up an image of a crackling fire.

"Sorry, this is the best I can do." He shrugs.

I walk to him, wrapping my arms around his waist as I look up into his eyes. "I think it's perfect. Thank you."

"You deserve this and so much more, Krissy. I'm sorry none of those other jerks realized that before." He wraps his arms around me, bringing back the feeling of comfort and safety I haven't felt with anyone else before.

"You can't possibly say that. You've only known me a few hours."

Is it possible he feels the same connection I do? There's no way. This doesn't happen. Especially not to me. I don't meet someone by accident and fall madly in love with them.

Is that what I'm doing? Falling in love? On Christmas Eve? With a stranger?

"I know it's crazy, but you're special, babe. I could tell from the moment I saw you sitting at that table with your Christmas sweater and fur-lined boots."

My heart pounds in my chest at his words. Everything about tonight has been crazy, intense—magical. I want to believe this is real and not some eggnog-induced fantasy.

Needing confirmation this isn't a dream, I pull Brett's lips to mine, relishing in the whiskey's smoky taste on his tongue.

Nope, definitely real.

Chapter Six

BRETT

How can someone taste like a sugar cookie?

I don't know how it's possible, but every taste of her gets sweeter and sweeter.

Not wanting to wait another moment, I place my hands on her ass like I've be thinking about all night, lift her into the air and carry her the few quick steps to the bed I've created for us. I smile as we continue to kiss, loving the way she immediately wraps her legs around my waist as I lift her.

Trailing my lips down the column of her neck, I lower us both to the ground. I can't get over how soft her skin is. How she smells like sugar cookies and magic. Sliding my hand along her thigh, with her legs still wrapped firmly around me, I squeeze her tighter as she arches her back, pressing her chest to mine.

I take the invitation and continue on. Sliding my hand under the bottom of her sweater, I pull it up over her head and throw it to the side. I hold back a chuckle as I look down at the holly patterned bra that lays underneath, barely containing her luscious breasts. "How fitting."

An adorable blush crosses her cheeks. "It's silly, I know."

"No, it's cute, and I love it. I wouldn't expect anything less."

"You don't think it's silly?" she asks with a flirty lilt to her question.

"Not even a little." I lower my head, sucking a nipple into my mouth through the fabric.

"Oooh," Krissy gasps, grabbing my hair as she squeezes her legs tighter around my hips. "I'm—uh—happy to help revive your holiday spirit."

It takes everything in me not to rip off the offending fabric that lay between us and thrust into her right now. I need to claim her. Make her mine. Make her moan like that as I fill her.

"You've revived a lot more than that," I growl as my lips trace down her skin, working on the button of her black pants. Sliding the zipper down, I smirk at the matching panties. I nibble at the skin just above the panty line, causing her body to jerk, a laugh tearing out of her. "Oh, you're ticklish too, huh?"

"No, please," Krissy laughs breathlessly. Her laughter quickly turns to more as I place my mouth on her fabric-covered mound, sucking her tight bud.

Slipping further down her body, I take off her boots and pants, with her panties following in one swift motion. Leaving her in only her holiday-themed bra. My hands slide along her silky skin, making their way up her stomach and through the valley of her breasts. I quickly undo the clasp, holding her gaze as I go. I want to see every thought, every emotion, that crosses her beautiful face as we do this. I want to make sure that she never remembers another douchebag that's ever made her feel bad for expressing what she wanted.

I throw her bra onto her pile of clothes, bracing myself on my hands above her as I trail my gaze down her body. "You're so beautiful."

Krissy smiles mischievously, running her hands up my

stomach and under my shirt. She doesn't say anything, just works her way at taking off every inch of my clothing, just as I did to her. My body tightens under her touch. I'm afraid that with every passing stroke along my skin, I'll explode. That I'll pounce on her and take what my body craves. But she deserves more than that. She deserves a night to remember in the lights of the Christmas tree.

My skin burns as she wraps her legs around my waist, pulling me closer. I close my eyes and relish in the feel of her body wrapped around mine. It's been so long since I've had more than a one-night stand with a woman. I've nearly forgotten how overwhelming the emotional side could be. Every other time I was just scratching an itch. Relieving stress. But I knew from the moment I saw Krissy, she wasn't that. This is more, and it both thrills and scares the fuck out of me.

Lowering my mouth to her nipple again, I suck in her stiff peak, alternating between nipping and sucking as my hand trails down lower. "Damn, angel. All of this for me?"

Incoherent words pass Krissy's lips as I pump my fingers in and out of her, circling the spot she craves the most. When I press on her bud, she arches her back and nearly flies off our makeshift bed. Her breathing increases, a slight hitch to it with every pass of my thumb.

I can feel myself throbbing. The need to be inside her is so overwhelming I almost give in, but not yet. It's not my turn. Right now is about Krissy and living out her fantasy of making love by the tree.

I almost stop as the words cross my mind.

Making love.

I've never made love with a woman before. Not really. One-night stands? Most certainly. But made love? No. That involves emotions I haven't felt in a very long time. Even then, I'm not sure that you could describe what Veronica and I did as 'making love.'

"Brett?" Her questioning tone brings me back to Krissy.

I can give her this. I can give her tonight. I don't know what the feelings are that I have for Krissy, but I'm pretty sure they are stronger than I've ever felt since Veronica.

But no, I won't think about her. Not now.

Looking down at the Christmas goddess beneath me, I'm dazed at how beautiful she is in nothing but the glow of the tree light. Her blonde curls sparkle in the twinkling lights, making her look even more like the angel I know she is.

If only I deserved her.

I lower my mouth to hers, drowning myself in a kiss to push out the unwelcome thoughts of my past. Her nails scratch down my back as she laps at my mouth, riding my hand. It's the hottest experience I've ever had, and I haven't even entered her yet.

"Come on, baby," I growl. "Let me feel you."

"Oh, Brett!" she yells as she lets go, throwing her head back and squeezing my fingers as she rides out her high.

Not wasting a moment after she comes down, I reach for my jeans, pull out the condom from my wallet, and rip the foil between my teeth. Krissy giggles as she takes the foil from my mouth, removing the latex and throwing the wrapper to the side. I don't even try to hide the groan that comes out of my mouth as she rolls the condom over me at a slow pace that is pure torture.

"Babe," I grind out between my teeth, using every ounce of restraint I have not to push her hands aside and sink into her like I really want to.

"I've got you," she purrs, pulling it down the last inch.

"Thank fuck." Grabbing her wrists, I place them above her head, causing her to gasp. "I'll be gentle. We'll do what you want. I just really need to feel you right now."

With her big, blue eyes shining up at me, she nods as I hold both her hands in one of mine, the other tracing soft lines down her body. My fingertips trace over the stiff peaks of her nipples, pinching and soothing as I brush over her soft breasts.

Emotion I barely recognize rushes through my body as I run my finger down her rib cage. Excitement? Trepidation? It's more than just pure physical lust. Nothing about what I feel for Krissy is normal, or like anything I've ever experienced before.

I watch her eyes close as she shifts underneath me, causing me to focus on the sensitive areas of her silky skin. She's so beautiful. So pure. She's given herself to me freely, trusting me in a way I don't deserve.

Pushing down the overwhelming emotion, I grab myself in my hand, looking back up her body. I see nothing but bliss on her face as I brace myself between her legs, rubbing myself against her entrance. Her purr turns into more as I sink in, going slower than I ever thought could be possible. I need to know this is what she wants, and she's feeling nothing but the same ecstasy I am being with her.

Giving into my urge, I fill her to the hilt, letting go of her hands and brace myself above her as I begin to move. Krissy wraps her legs around my waist, pushing her heels into my ass, spurring me on with every thrust.

I know I'm not going to last long. Not with this angel under me. Squeezing me. Rocking her hips into me. Certainly not with her working whatever Christmas magic she brought into my bar with her tonight.

I bring my hand between our joined bodies, strumming her as I pick up the pace. I need to draw one more release out of her before I take my own. "Come on, angel," I growl. "I need to feel you."

"Oh, Brett!" She screams as she lets go. Pride fills my chest, knowing I made her come so hard this small elf screamed louder than I bet she has in her life. I'm also thrilled I don't have any neighbours close enough to hear. That scream is for me, and me alone.

I let myself follow her with a grunt, releasing the stress of the last six months and feeling it wash away. I lower my body to rest on my forearms, making sure not to crush her, but needing to give myself a moment to collect my breath.

In this moment, I feel closer to her than I've ever felt to anyone. I don't want to roll over and count the minutes until she leaves the bed like I usually do after a night like this. I want to take in every moment, remember every happy sigh that comes out of her mouth. Remember the way her body glows in the dim light of the Christmas tree. I take my finger and blindly trace the curve of her cheek as I drop my forehead to her shoulder. I need to remember everything about this moment.

I wrap my arms around her and roll us to our sides, tucking her in tightly against me. With her back flush to my front, we lay here in happy silence, falling asleep to the twinkling lights and the soft sound of Christmas carols. I can't stop the lazy smile that crosses my face as I hold her. Just as I can't stop thinking that maybe it was a Christmas miracle that brought her to me.

Chapter Seven

KRISSY

I feel as if I'm still dreaming when I wake up in Brett's arms. His warm, hard body is pressed against my back, his thick arm wrapped possessively around my waist. I smile to myself as I snuggle into him further, loving everything about this moment. The gentle breeze of his breath on my neck, the way his arm holds me tight like he isn't ready to let me go.

The fireplace on the TV still roars to life with the occasional hand coming to stoke the fire. Elvis' smooth voice plays softly in the background.

A perfect Christmas morning.

"It's too early," Brett's groggy voice sounds from behind me as he pulls me in closer, rubbing his short, scruffy beard against my shoulder. "Go back to sleep."

"And a bah humbug to you, too," I chuckle, placing my arms over his.

"No bah humbug. Just sleepy. Shhh."

I laugh at how cute morning Brett is. I like this side of him. I bet it's a side no one ever gets to see. I also selfishly hope I'm the only one that gets to see it.

Craning my neck, I look out the window behind us to see

the snow has stopped, and the sun is shining brightly through the window. I close my eyes and wiggle my butt further into him, trying to get as close as possible. I would love to get a little more sleep and enjoy the feeling of being with him, but the incessant buzzing of my phone stops me.

Brett groans, making me giggle. For such a big, strong man, he's now reduced to pouting. I don't have to guess that he's not much of a morning person.

Carefully prying myself out of his arms, I grab his discarded button-up shirt, wrapping it around myself as I look for my purse. Finding it on the couch where I'd thrown it last night, I dig out my phone, smiling at the number of missed messages in my group chat with my family.

MOM

Merry Christmas! Can't wait to see all your smiling faces today! *smiling emoji* *Christmas tree emoji* *Santa emoji*

TRENT

Merry Christmas, Mom. Can't wait for your turkey! *turkey emoji* *licking lips emoji*

WYATT

Of course, all you're concerned about is food.

Has anyone heard from Krissy? It's not like her not to send a million Christmas gifs by now.

TRENT

She had that date last night. Hopefully not another fuckwitt.

MOM

Trent, language.

Date? What date? On Christmas Eve? Oh, it's like it was meant to be!

WYATT

Mom, don't get ahead of yourself.

Merry Christmas, Mom! Yes, I had a date. I'll tell you all about it later.

MOM

Do you want to bring him? There's always room!

WYATT

Mom, he probably has somewhere to be.

I'll talk to him and let you know. Talk later! *kiss emoji* *Santa emoji*

WYATT

No wonder Dad refuses to take part in this chat.

I smile, placing the phone back into my purse, and turning back to Brett. He's propped up on his elbow, head resting on his hand. The blanket has fallen to his waist, leaving his well-toned chest on display. The delicious smile he's giving me makes me ache for him all over again.

"What's that look for?" I walk back to him, crawling back under the covers.

"You made the most adorable face when you were looking at your screen." Reaching up, he tucks a strand of my hair behind my ear.

"It was just my family wishing each other a Merry Christmas and wondering why I haven't inundated them with Christmas gifs yet." I feel a rush of heat to my cheeks with my admission. It's true, I would usually wake on Christmas morning and send as many festive gifs as I could find driving my brothers crazy, but I have something to distract me this morning.

"Hmm, I wonder if that reason could convince you to stay

in bed all day," he says, unbuttoning his shirt I'm wearing, kissing behind the trail of his fingers.

"I'd love to, but I have to go to my parents'." I place my hands on his shoulders and arch into him as he kisses his way down my chest. "You're invited, by the way."

Brett stops, snapping his head up to mine. "What?"

"I mean, no pressure, but if you're free, you're welcome to come with me to Christmas dinner." He looks at me for a moment before jumping up like our makeshift bed is on fire. He grabs his jeans and stomps into them. "Brett, what's wrong?"

"I, uh, just remembered a lot of things I have to do today," he says, not looking at me. He paces in front of his kitchen, running his hands through his hair.

"Brett, what's going on?" I hold his shirt together, standing as I watch him continue to pace. "It's Christmas Day, and there was a snowstorm. What do you have to do?"

"Look, this was fun and all, but I have stuff to do." He pushes the curtains aside and looks out the window, a streak of sunlight lighting up his face. "The streets are plowed, and it stopped snowing. Let me go dig out your car, and you can get on your way." Without looking at me, he disappears down the hallway.

I have no idea what happened to cause such a dramatic turn. Was it impulsive to invite him to my family dinner on Christmas? Probably, but I also hate the idea of him being alone today. I let my desire to spend more time with him override my rational thought. Of course he doesn't want to come with me. To my parents' place. On Christmas. His words from the night before flow over me, making me realize just what an idiot I'm being. He's not into holidays and he doesn't have family. I know I overstepped here, and I've obviously made him panic.

Fighting back the tears from being cast aside, I pull my clothes out from the heap by the tree. Reaching out, I run my fingertips along the silver garland, thinking back to when we had decorated it. I want that Brett back. The one that laughed and let down his gruff, grinch exterior. But now the grump is back, and I'm not sure what to do about it.

"Get dressed. I'll have your car ready to go in fifteen," he says as he comes out of the hallway, fully dressed in a winter jacket and boots.

"Brett, I'm sorry. I wasn't thinking…." I take a step forward, holding my hand out to place it on his chest, but he steps away, moving toward the door.

"Fifteen minutes, Krissy." Without another word or glance my way, he's gone.

I sigh as I turn back to the tree, letting my gaze rest on it as I whisper "Merry Christmas" to myself.

Chapter Eight

BRETT

I find the act of digging the snow and tossing it to the side oddly therapeutic. There's something about the mindless work that helps exhaust me both mentally and physically.

Saying Krissy shocked me by inviting me to her parents' place is an understatement. What guy in his right mind would agree to meet her family for the first time on Christmas Day? Especially when they had just met the night before. That's a disaster waiting to happen.

I thought I had moved on enough—recovered enough—from my ex-girlfriend, Veronica. In the beginning, she'd been everything I wanted. We were having fun, going with the flow. No commitments. No drama. Then one day, she decided it was time for me to meet her parents. Move in together. She started talking about getting married. All the things I swore I never wanted or needed. The thought of staying in one place too long always felt suffocating to me, and I did everything I could to avoid it.

Veronica hadn't handled it well when I told her I didn't do commitments. She'd cried, begged, and pleaded with me to stay, for us to make a go of it, but in the end, I just couldn't.

When she finally realized I had made up my mind, she had gone out of her way to make my life difficult. She racked up bills on my store credit around town, knowing everyone knew we were together. She sabotaged some jobs I had lined up in other towns, calling behind my back, saying I was no longer interested. In the end, I left with just enough money to get out of town and buy The Lucky Dog, and that was only possible because the owner was retiring and wanted out as quick as possible.

Now, after only a night, Krissy was starting with the same.

She swept into my bar like a holiday blizzard, clouding my judgement and making me forget I'd sworn myself to a life of bachelorhood. She started making me want things I've never wanted before, but now, in the light of the day, I realize I wasn't meant for that life. I can't let myself think I could fit in somewhere, settle down, and have a family like everyone else.

A family. Where the fuck did that come from?

Digging the shovel into the snow harder than necessary, I work until my muscles scream at me to take a break. I don't need to take my anger out on the mound of snow that buried Krissy's car, but it was my only alternative right now. It is, after all, the car she needs to get in and drive as far away from The Lucky Dog as quickly as she can.

It's not just for my own benefit, but for hers as well. I'm not any good for her. I'm a drifter that's never had a real home. Never had anywhere I could call mine. Buying the pub has been my first attempt at settling down for any period of time, and what happened? I messed it all up in the first couple of months.

"Brett!" Krissy's raised voice trails from the door. "Who do you think you are storming out on me like that?"

Sighing, I stick the shovel into the snow and survey the street, which is thankfully deserted. The last thing I need is an audience witnessing me be the jerk of the year. "We don't need to do this, Krissy."

"Like hell, we don't!" My sweet Christmas angel is gone. Before me is all fire and brimstone. "You can't just turn off the switch like that. What about everything you said last night?"

"I must have been caught up in whatever Christmas voodoo you brought into the pub with you. Nothing about that guy was me."

"So, you lied?" I hate hearing the hurt that is laced into her words. Hate seeing the frown on her face as the realization dawns on her. "You said all that just to sleep with me?"

My body screams 'no, don't let her believe that!' but my brain doesn't listen. My brain tells me to save both of us a lifetime of hurt and to just let her move on and forget about me. "Yes."

Krissy gasps as she raises her hand to cover her mouth. "You can't mean that," she whispers.

Holding back a cringe, I watch how her cute red nails contrast with her porcelain skin, cheeks reddened by the cold. My heart knows Krissy isn't anything like Veronica. It knows that there might be a possibility of something other than a cold, lonely life with this woman. But my mind? It's telling me it's not possible. A life like that just isn't in the cards for me. And dammit, I believe it.

My heart screams to take it back, to say I didn't mean it. I want to do anything that stops those tears from welling in her eyes, but I can't.

I'm a coward. I know it, but I've gone too far.

Looking down at the pile of snow at my feet, I know I've shovelled more than enough for her to get out. It's stopped snowing, and the streets are plowed. There isn't anything keeping her here with me. "I do. Look, we had fun, and that's it. Don't read more into this than it is."

"But everything you said about the Christmas magic. About how it was special."

The quiver in her voice makes me want to scoop her up and bring her inside, kissing away all the doubt and hurt in her eyes. But I can't. I harden myself, adding a firmness to my voice I almost don't recognize. "There's no such thing as magic."

She sniffs as a tear runs down her cheek. "Why are you doing this?"

"Goodbye, Krissy."

"You're a selfish asshole." With a final wipe at her tears, Krissy hitches her bag higher on her shoulder as she storms past me. Throwing her door open, she tosses her bag inside, standing straighter and narrowing her eyes at me. "And Bah Humbug to you, too. I hope you enjoy your holiday *alone*."

Slamming the door, she starts her car and takes off, getting away from me as fast as possible. I don't blame her. I deserve that.

I stand helpless on the street as I watch her car take off down the road. "Jackass," I mutter, kicking the mound of snow before yanking the shovel out and stomping inside.

What I need now is a stiff drink, angry music, and to be alone.

Chapter Nine

KRISSY

Staring at the flickering flames in the fireplace, I can't help but wonder what went so wrong. Last night was the best night of my life. I thought maybe all my dating struggles were finally coming to an end. That maybe Mack standing me up was the best thing to happen to me, since it led me to Brett. Instead, all I got was heartache and a less-than-jolly Christmas.

Taking a sip of the coffee in my hands, I wince at how cold it's gotten.

How long have I been standing here?

"So," Trent says as he throws himself on the couch beside me. "Are you going to tell me what happened, or do I need to beat up every single guy in Whiskey Falls until I find out the truth?"

I glare at him over my mug. "You wouldn't do that."

"Try me," he says with his signature smile, which implies there's about a fifty-fifty chance he means what he said.

"Nothing to tell. I got stood up, ended up snowed in with someone, and it didn't work out. That's it." I turn my attention back to the fire, taking another sip of my now-iced coffee, trying not to wince.

"That's not it. I know you, Krissy. You don't do hookups or one-night stands. Something else happened." Trent leans forward, resting his elbows on his knees as he playfully knocks his shoulder into mine. "You can tell me."

"You want me to tell my big brother about a guy that broke my heart? Yeah, nice try. Nothing good ever comes of that."

"Ah, see. We're getting somewhere. And it's just me; it's not like you're telling Wyatt."

"Telling Wyatt what?" a deep, booming voice rings out behind me.

I sigh, placing my mug on the coffee table next to me and putting my head in my hands. The last thing I need is for my older brothers to find out about Brett. Who knows what they'd do.

"Nothing!" I exclaim as I stand, turning to face Wyatt as he stands behind the couch. "There's nothing to tell you because nothing happened. Now, leave it alone!" I can't help how my voice raises or how I clench my fists at my sides. I don't want my brothers finding out about the colossal mistake I made in trusting Brett or falling for his smooth words. I feel nothing but shame as I think back, seeing that he's not any better than the other men I've met off that fucking dating app.

No, this mistake was on me. I chose to believe him. I looked past all the things I would normally see in a lying asshole and was blinded by what I thought was Christmas magic.

Stupid Krissy.

Also, damn Brett. Damn him for getting to me and ruining my favourite holiday.

"This isn't 'nothing,' Krissy-Bear. Something happened," Trent says, using the nickname he gave me when we were kids. He knows I melt a little toward him when he uses it.

Damn Trent, too.

I close my eyes and let out a deep breath, stilling the raging fire that's burning in my chest. I wish my brothers would just leave it alone, but another part of me wants to get it all out; to tell someone. Even if that someone would go to the ends of the Earth to kick the living shit out of anyone that hurt me. I've always been very close with Trent and Wyatt, but they are still my older brothers, and they can be very protective.

Steeling myself, I open my eyes and face them. Wyatt looks at me with concern as he crosses his arms over his chest while Trent sits casually on the couch with his arm resting over the back of it.

"Fine. I went to the Lucky Dog Pub last night to meet up with a guy I met online. He didn't show. I got snowed in and spent the night with the new owner. He woke up, decided relationships weren't his thing, and I left. Happy now?"

"No, we aren't 'happy now,'" Wyatt grumbles as he narrows his eyes at me. "Who is this fucker? Did he lead you on? Do we need to kick his ass?"

"No, I don't want you to kick anyone's ass," I retort, rolling my eyes. "What I want is to forget last night ever happened. I made an error in judgement, and I won't be doing it again."

"That's not you, Krissy. You don't make these errors. Wyatt and I do all the time," he starts, when Wyatt interrupts him.

"Speak for yourself, jackass." Wyatt smacks Trent on the back of the head.

"But you don't," Trent finishes, not even flinching at Wyatt's antics but giving a good eye roll. "Plus, you haven't been yourself today. I haven't seen you sing along to one Christmas carol; you barely cracked a smile while opening presents. There's nothing 'happy' about this situation."

"So? I'm allowed to not be happy once in a while." I cross my arms over my chest as I stare them down. I can admit I had to stop myself from stomping like a toddler as I narrow my eyes at them. I love my brothers, but they aren't helping my mood at the moment.

"You're allowed not to be happy, but this is your favourite day of the year. If some asswipe upset you and took that away, then yes, he deserves to have his ass kicked." Wyatt balls his fists as he rests them on the back of the couch. It's not often he gets this riled up, and I hate seeing him this way.

I drop my arms and draw out a breath. "Look, I appreciate you caring, but I'm fine—or, I will be." That earns me glares from both of them. "Why don't we watch a movie while Mom finishes up dinner? I'll even suck it up and pretend Die Hard is a Christmas movie."

"Hmph, now I know you aren't feeling alright," Wyatt scoffs, taking a seat on the opposite side of the couch as Trent.

Sitting in between them, I take each one of their hands and give them a squeeze. "Thanks, guys. I love you."

"And we love you, sis," Trent says, pulling me over and giving me a kiss on the top of my head. "Now, go and get us some Die Hard. Yippee-Ki-ya mo-"

"Yeah, yeah, yeah. I'm on it." I push up from the couch and grab the remote.

While I might have woken this morning thinking the day would go differently, I'm glad for my brothers. Maybe the holiday can be salvaged after all.

Chapter Ten

BRETT

"So, then the missus goes and tells them they should come back for the rodeo. Can you believe it?" Tom Wilkins complains as he takes a sip from his longneck. I watch as his withered, darkened face scrunches up in disdain. "She knows I can't stand her cousins, and she goes and invites them for the busiest time of the year."

"Maybe it'll give you a reason to sneak out; avoid them," Archer Decker replies as he takes a sip of his beer. Though decades younger than Tom, he seems to always lend an ear to anyone willing to talk.

I only half listen as I stand behind the bar, wiping a glass. I can't stop thinking about Krissy and how much of a jerk I was to her yesterday. My head also throbs, thanks to the amount of whiskey I drank trying to forget the whole ordeal.

Only I can't. I will never be able to forget the feel of her skin or the way her body writhed beneath mine. I shake my head, trying to clear the images of her from my brain, ignoring the rush of heat that bursts through my veins. She's a dream, an oasis in the lonely desert I've created for myself. I don't deserve the right to think about her, just like she doesn't deserve how I've treated her.

The thud of the heavy door slamming open breaks me from my spinning thoughts, snapping my attention to the two angry men stomping their way through my bar. My body goes on high alert. I know they aren't here for a drink. They are here to cause trouble. Now, I need to find out why.

"What can I do for you, gentleman?" I put the glass and towel down on the bar in front of me. I hope I don't need to use my hands, but I've learned it's always good to be ready.

"Are you the owner of this place?" the bigger, and grumpier, looking one asks. He stands a good four inches taller than me, which says a lot. With his arms crossed over his chest, he flexes his biceps, which look like they're trying to escape from the denim covering them.

"I am." I place my hands on the cool wood in front of me. The last thing I want is trouble, and these two look like trouble.

"I don't know what you've done, son, but you're in for it now," Tom chuckles into his beer.

Not knowing what the old man means, I focus on the two pissed-off giants in front of me. "How can I help you?"

"We're here about our sister," the other says. While slightly shorter and leaner than the first man, he's still just as intimidating, but they don't scare me. I can hold my own, but that doesn't mean I want to get into a brawl in my own bar.

Wait, sister?

Oh, shit. They must be the brothers Krissy was texting.

"Yeah, we just want a word about how you treated her the other night," the smaller one says.

Smaller giant, more like.

"You messed with Krissy?" Archer puts down his beer, body tensing like he's ready to join in on the action.

"Woah, hold up." I place my hands in front of me in surrender. "I didn't mean to hurt her," *exactly*, "it just didn't work out."

"That's not what we heard. We heard you lured her into

your bed and then discarded her. On Christmas Day," the taller one spits out.

"You what?" Archer shoots up from his stool.

"Stay out of this, Archer," I warn, giving him a glare.

"They hell I will. Krissy is a friend." He moves to stand with the brothers. "If Wyatt said you did that, I believe him, and you're going to need to explain yourself."

This isn't how I imagined my start in Whiskey Falls. I wanted to come in, lay low, and run a decent bar for the locals that was a quiet place to get a drink. Instead, I just had to come in guns blazing, making a mess of it all.

"I'm sorry things happened the way they did. I truly didn't want Krissy to get hurt, but I'm not the guy for her. I can't be the guy for her."

"Well, she sure thought you were. If you're going to last in this town, I suggest you make it right with her. Everyone in Whiskey Falls loves Krissy, which means when they find out about what you did, they will make it very hard for you to stay. Do you understand?" Wyatt asks.

Make it right with her. If only it were that easy. Judging by how she left the day before, I'm sure the last thing she wants to do is talk to me again. My heart tells me I need to take the chance, that I need to push in order to get my thoughts in order and do what I know I have to do. I miss Krissy, as crazy as it sounds after only being together for a short period of time. I'm miserable knowing that I've had a glimpse of what my life could be, and it came in the form of happiness brought by a bubbly blonde elf.

"What makes you think she even wants to talk to me?" I ask, looking between the three men in front of me.

"She'll be madder than a wet hen, but she'll talk," the shorter one says. He drops his arms, no longer looking like he was going to beat me to a pulp. His voice lowers as he continues. "You ruined her Christmas, man. If you can ever get her to forgive you for that, you can get her to forgive you for whatever jackass shit you said to her."

I ruined her Christmas? The thought of her spending her favourite holiday sad guts me. I know she was mad when she left, and maybe it was naïve of me to think she would just get over it when I know full well Krissy isn't like other girls.

"Trent, don't give him ideas," Wyatt snaps.

"What? You saw her. He doesn't look much happier about the situation, either," Trent throws his arm in my direction before pointing his finger at me. "You're still in the doghouse, by the way."

"I know." I throw my hands up in front of me.

"So, what are you going to do about it?" Archer asks.

That's the million-dollar question, isn't it? What am going to do about it? What do I *want* to do about it? Do I still believe Krissy is different from Veronica? Is it possible she's every-thing I've never dared to dream about having before? Of course. But am I ready to *do* anything about it? That's the question.

If I'm going to grovel, it's not going to be because of the town or men in front of me. It's going to be because I'm ready to try with Krissy. To be in it for the long haul.

Looking around the room, I take a deep breath and try to figure out what I want. Do I listen to my head that tells me it's not worth it? That I'll only end up hurting us both in the end. Or do I listen to my heart? My heart tells me it's time to let go of the walls I've put up. That I need to let go of the damage Veronica did and see Krissy for who she is. A beautiful, amazing woman that can give me everything I didn't think I could ever have.

Looking back at the guys, I drop my shoulders along with all the stress that has built up in my body. "I'm going to need some help."

Chapter Eleven

KRISSY

I can only imagine what I look like right now, sitting at the counter of my Christmas store, looking out the window but not really seeing what's in front of me. People mill through the main streets of Whiskey Falls, enjoying the relaxed time between Christmas and New Years when time ceases to exist. But for me, all I have is time.

The post-Christmas rush has ended for me. No one was out rushing to buy the deals or the last-minute gifts, which means I have all the time in the world to think about Brett. I wonder how I could have been so stupid to think that he would be any different, that he would have wanted me for more than just a one-night stand. I've always been good at picking them out before, but Brett clouded my judgement, making me think he wanted more than he really did.

Embarrassment washes over me when I think of how my brothers reacted to the news. How they immediately responded with anger, which is ironic if they looked at how many one-night stands and hookups they've had.

"Freaking double standards," I mutter to myself.

While my brothers aren't mad at me, it doesn't make it any easier knowing where their anger lies. While I'm mad at

Brett and disappointed in myself, I don't have any ill will toward him. Not anymore, anyway. After another sleepless night, I decided we both have to live in Whiskey Falls, so there's no point in staying mad at him. I can avoid him. I spent however long he'd been in town before the other night not seeing him, and I can do it again. It'll be hard in a town like ours, but it's doable.

The bell above the door rings, bringing me out of my less-than-stellar daydream. I smile at our local delivery carrier as he walks through the door. "Good morning, Hank. What brings you in today?"

"You have a package, Krissy," he says, placing a box on the counter between us.

"I didn't order anything." I look at the package suspiciously.

"That makes it even more exciting." Hank gives me a wink. "Happy Holidays, Krissy. Enjoy your surprise."

"Yeah, bye, Hank," I say mindlessly to the older man as he leaves. I turn the package around. "No return address. That's odd."

Ripping the packing tape off the top, I open the flaps and look inside. Three boxes, wrapped carefully in green and red paper, are stacked on top of each other, each with a number on it.

I carefully pull out the top box with a '1' written in bold, black lettering. Curiosity gets the better of me as I unwrap it, revealing a white box. Flipping the lid, inside I see a wooden ornament; a reindeer with sad looking eyes holding a banner reading 'I'm sorry.'

Growing even more curious, I move to the box with the '2,' ripping open the paper and finding a similar white box. This ornament inside is in the shape of the Grinch holding up a sign reading 'I'm an idiot.'

I can't help the laugh that escapes my lips. I think I'm starting to get an idea of who my mystery gift-giver might be.

Reaching in, I pull out the last gift marked with a '3.'

Ripping the paper to find another white box, I open it and smile at the third and final gift. Two bees wearing elf hats are kissing, holding a banner that says 'Would you bee my elf?'

I giggle, covering my mouth with my fingers as the door to my shop opens; this time, it's the man himself standing in front of me. I gasp as he closes the distance between us, holding a gorgeous, deep red poinsettia in his hands.

"Hi, Krissy."

"Brett. Did you do this?"

"Too much?" he asks, a tint of pink hits his cheeks. He's the most handsome man I've ever seen, and his embarrassment and hesitation only make him that much more attractive.

"That depends. What does this mean?" The last of my anger has melted away with every ornament I opened. I want to hear him explain this to me, and this time, I will listen without the lens of Christmas magic.

"It means that I'm an idiot and I never should have said those things to you. I never meant to hurt you, Krissy. Not really. I also didn't lie to you the night we were together. I meant every word I said. The only time I lied was the next morning." He places the plant on the counter between us.

"So, why did you do it?" Frustration rears his head again as I listen to his words, hearing that he purposefully lied to me. "Why tell me that none of it meant anything to you when it did?"

"I was scared. You make me feel things I've never felt before. You're forever, Krissy, and I've never had anything that felt like forever before."

"So, what made you change your mind?" I can't help how my voice raises, or how my hands clench at my sides.

"Your brothers," he looks down sheepishly. "And Archer."

"Archer?" My eyes widen in surprise as I watch him. "What does Archer have to do with this?"

"He was in the pub when your brothers came blazing in." His eyes burrow into mine. The man in front of me is so unlike the one I met the other night. This Brett is hesitant. Less self-assured. "You have the town ready to fight for you."

"Small town. You should know that. I'm assuming Logan Creek is the same."

"Yeah." He holds my gaze before flicking his attention to the ornaments on the counter. "I guess I just never let myself realize that before."

"Why not?" I whisper, letting my body relax. I can see the war brewing inside of him. Something happened, and I need to know what that something is.

"I lost my parents when I was young. The town tried to be there for me, but I was angry and shut them out. That's when I started moving to where the jobs were. As soon as anything got too real, I left."

"And now?" I'm almost afraid to hear where this is going.

"Now," he says as she takes a step toward me. "I want to stay. I want to see what it's really like to be accepted by a small town and a beautiful woman. That is, if she'll forgive me for being the worst Grinch that ever lived on Christmas Day."

"I guess that depends." I walk around the counter toward him, not taking my eyes from his. He tracks me as I move, turning his body slightly toward me.

"On?"

"Whether you tell me the truth about what made you scared Christmas morning. I know I shouldn't have invited you. I wasn't thinking. All I knew was I wanted to spend more time with you, and I hated the thought of you being alone, especially during a holiday. Of course, you wouldn't have wanted to come to meet my family the day after we met. But there's more to it, isn't there?"

"You're right." He lets out a haggard breath and runs his fingers through his hair. "I was in Clearwater before I came here for about three years. During that time, I met Veronica. She seemed like she wanted what I did, until after a couple of months, she pressed for more. She wanted me to meet her family, move in, get married. All things I told her up front I didn't want."

My heart drops as I listen to Brett speak. "Oh, Brett..." I grab his hands, squeezing them, letting him know I'm here for him.

"When I told her that I think it's best if we end it, she flipped out. She started crying and screaming, saying I led her on. She did some things that led to me getting out of town as quickly as possible." He looks down at our joined hands for a moment before bringing his deep blue eyes back to mine. "I shouldn't have, but when you mentioned going to your family's place, I panicked. I knew I was being an ass, but I couldn't help it."

"I wish you would have told me that the other day."

"I wish I did, too." The corner of his mouth ticks up in a sad smile. "I'm so sorry, Krissy. You didn't deserve anything I did. I hope that you can consider forgiving me and giving us another chance. I've been so miserable without you."

"Well, you are my grinch..."

Brett chuckles. "Yeah, I guess I am."

"So the question now is whether or not your heart has grown three sizes." I place my hands on his chest, feeling the cold of this leather jacket contrasting with the heat rolling off his body. Pure desire pools in his eyes as he looks at me, placing his hands on my waist.

"Oh, it did, and then some. I think I've also rid myself of all the ghosts of the past."

"Wrong Christmas story," I giggle.

"The facts are still the same." Reaching up, he brushes my hair off my face, tucking it behind my ear. "I'm so sorry, Krissy. I'll never lie or hide my feelings from you again. That, I promise you."

I search his eyes, finding nothing but the truth. "I believe you."

"Oh, thank God," he says, dropping his forehead to mine and closing his eyes.

I clutch the leather of his jacket in my hands, pulling him closer to me.

"Brett?" My voice is breathless as I whisper his name.

"Yeah?" He opens his eyes.

"Kiss me."

He doesn't hesitate as he lowers his lips to mine. Just like that, all the pain and fear from the last few days melts away as we get lost in each other. I know I've found what I've always been looking for. It doesn't come with an app or with a book. It comes with raw, real emotions and fear. It comes with a realness that I wouldn't have found other than in the most authentic way possible, and with magic I would only ever find in Whiskey Falls.

Epilogue

BRETT

One Year Later

I put the last glass away, throwing the towel over my shoulder as I let out a sigh of relief. It's been a long day of providing food and drink for the lonely people of Whiskey Falls. I wish more than anything Krissy could have been by my side today. Not just because the rush was busier than I expected, but because I feel like I've barely seen her since the Christmas season started, even though we now live together in the apartment above the bar. She's been so busy with her shop and making ornaments. She's been falling asleep before I'm done down here and she's gone before I wake up.

Thankfully, not for much longer.

Tonight is Christmas Eve. One year since she walked into my bar and turned my life upside down. It also means tomorrow is Christmas Day, both of our businesses will be closed, and the only obligation we have is dinner at her parents' place.

That's right, the very same dinner that nearly prevented us from even starting a relationship, thanks to my stupidity.

I smile as I look around the bar, decorated with the twinkling lights and Christmas trees—plural—placed strategically around the room. Krissy squealed with joy when I told her she could decorate the place however she wanted. The next thing I knew, a trunk-full of bags filled to the brim with lights, wreaths, and decorations had been bought.

The Lucky Dog Pub isn't known for being the classiest place in Whiskey Falls, but somehow, Krissy had made it look like one.

"Hey there, handsome," her soft voice purrs behind me. I didn't hear her come in through the back, like she usually does.

"Hey yourself, beautiful." I turn, taking her in my arms. I inhale the unique scent of sugar and vanilla that seems to come naturally to her. "I missed you today."

"I missed you, too." She wraps her arms around me, and we stay like that in the silence of the bar for a few moments. "How did it go today?"

"Good. Busy." I kiss the top of her head and pull back. "I'm all done here. Do you need me to grab anything from the car?" She had been doing some last-minute shopping when she could and usually had a trunkful of gifts for me to bring up when I had a lull with the customers. I would grumble about it, but I love that she's so caring and thoughtful with gift giving. I also love doing the little things like carrying them up for her.

"No, nothing today." She sinks into me for a moment longer before pulling away. "I couldn't get away from the store today. I think I have everything, anyway. What I really want more than anything is to go upstairs and enjoy Christmas Eve with you. Maybe watch White Christmas?"

"Anything you want, babe." I take one last look around the bar, making sure I've locked everything up for the night before guiding her upstairs.

She doesn't know it, but I've got a surprise waiting for her.

My heart pounds nearly as loud as our footsteps as we climb the stairs. I spent all morning getting everything just right, and now I'm nervous as hell for Krissy to see it.

Staying close behind her, I hold my breath as she unlocks the door and walks in, dropping her purse on the table next to us. At first she doesn't notice, and my heart drops thinking she's too tired. Maybe the timing is wrong. What was I thinking doing it on Christmas Eve after we'd both had a long and gruelling month of work?

"Do you want wine?" she asks, moving to the kitchen, completely bypassing the living room all together. It's an open concept room, so there's still the opportunity to see what I've done, but my mind races as she opens the fridge, pulling out a bottle of white.

"Uh, yeah." I can't put together any more words than that right now. A thin layer of sweat coats my forehead. I rub my sweaty palms on my jeans, my eyes zipping between Krissy and the scene awaiting her.

"What about dinner? I know we planned to throw something together, but I'm just so tired. Do you think Pete will still have pizza delivery this late?" She uncorks her wine, her back still to the living room.

"I'm sure we could talk him into it. Or I could go get it." Unlike last year, there isn't a blizzard outside. The roads are clear. Krissy isn't here for anyone other than me, thank God.

Now if only she would turn around and stop making me sweat like it's the middle of August.

I take a step further into the room, hoping to draw her attention away from the take-out menu and into the living room. I left a light on before I started work this morning, casting a light glow in the middle of the room. Twinkling lights hang on the tv and on the plastic tree. The same one I carried upstairs last year. I offered to get a new one, but Krissy refused, saying that was our tree and we were going to keep it forever.

I glance behind me, making sure the TV is turned on, the screen flickering with a flame giving the illusion of a fireplace.

Music! That's what I'm forgetting!

Keeping an eye on her to make sure I don't miss her seeing this for the first time, I tap on my phone, glancing away only to make sure I'm hitting the right play list. Michael Buble's smooth voice croons over my speakers as he and Idina Menzel sing 'Baby, It's Cold Outside.'

"Ahh, I love this song," Krissy's voice trails as she looks up at me, taking in what's behind me. "Brett? What's all this?"

I've recreated our first night together the best that I can. I have the soft glow of the Christmas lights. The fire. The music. I've even pulled our bedding onto the floor in front of the tree, just like that night a year ago.

"Come here, babe." I open my hand to her. I wait patiently as she puts her glass of wine down on the counter before making her way to me. My heart is pounding so hard in my chest I'd be surprised if she doesn't hear it.

It feels like an eternity before she places her hand in mine, taking her gaze off the setup and looking into my eyes. "What's going on?"

"Krissy, one year ago you blew into my bar and changed my life forever. I know it hasn't been smooth sailing, and that I'm not always the easiest to live with, but I want you to know that I love you, and I wouldn't change a single minute of it." I suck in a breath as I prepare myself for the next part.

This is something I never saw myself doing. I never thought about how a night like this would go. I could be doing this all wrong for all I know.

And I want this perfect for her.

I squeeze her hand before I drop down to one knee. Her gasp and the unshed tears that fill her eyes tell me I did a good job at keeping this a secret.

One point for me.

"Krissy, you're the love of my life. I never pictured myself spending the rest of my life with anyone—until I met you. You're everything I didn't know I needed. You make me smile when the rest of the world makes me curse. You let me feel vulnerable when everyone else needs me to be strong. You're..." I struggle to find the right word that describes her. But really, there was only one that fit. "Perfect."

"Oh, Brett." Her free hand shoots to her lips.

I let go of her other hand and pull the box out from my pocket. The green velvet has been burning a hole in my jeans all day. I'm surprised no one picked up on it.

Another gasp escapes her lips as I pop open the top, revealing the ring I picked out especially for her. One I knew would suit her perfectly. It's a one karat diamond set with smaller stones to form the shape of a snowflake.

"Krissy Winters. I'm asking you to be my wife. Marry me, angel."

"Yes, Brett! Yes, I'll be your wife!" Krissy launches herself at me, my arms barely making it around her waist as she pounces, causing us both to fall back onto the blanket. We're lost in each other as we kiss and laugh, barely breaking free long enough for me to slip the ring onto her finger.

"You've made me the happiest woman in the world, Brett Jansen."

"And you've made me the happiest man, my little elf." I run the tip of my nose along the bridge of hers, taking in her sweet, sugary scent.

"I guess I finally made a Christmas lover out of you, didn't I?" She looks over her shoulder at the setup I made.

"I don't know if I'd go that far." I brush my knuckle under her chin, dragging her attention back to me. "But I love having Christmas with you."

I don't let her respond as I crush my lips to hers.

Just like that night on the floor last Christmas, I spend

hours making love to her, showing her just how much she means to me. I may not have asked for a tiny elf to show up at my bar, changing my life forever, but I'll be forever grateful for my Christmas miracle.

Excerpt from Second Chance with a Country Star

CHAPTER ONE

Ella

"Ella, have you seen the documents for the Sampson file?" Dakota's voice rings out from her office next to my desk, laced with panic.

"I'm sure they're right in front of you," I chuckle as I stand, brushing down my skirt. My heels clack on the tile floor as I cross the reception area to her office, making me smile. I don't know what it is about that sound that makes me feel so satisfied, but it does. Like I'm really a grown up with a grown up job, which, of course I have been for quite a while now.

"I looked. Am I going crazy? I feel like I'm going crazy."

I feel bad for her as soon as I reach her door. There are papers all over her desk and boxes stacked high along one wall. She's been working on this case for six months, and it's a huge one for her. It's the first one she's had the lead on by herself since moving to Whiskey Falls, and all the partners are watching to see how she handles it.

I walk to her desk, scanning the folders that I know she's

probably looked at a million times. I sigh as I pick up the one she's looking for and hold it out to her. "Here you go."

"I swear that wasn't there a moment ago." She flops down into her leather chair, causing it to roll back slightly as she does. "Thank you. I don't know what I'd do without you, Ella."

"Well, it's a good thing you'll never have to find out." I smile, taking a seat in the chair across from her. "You're going to do great, you know? You know this case inside and out."

"That doesn't guarantee a win, though." She pinches the bridge of her nose, closing her eyes. "What if I can't do this, Ella?"

I slump back into my chair, thinking of the best way to approach this. I don't know what happened exactly, but Dakota hasn't been the same since the breakup with her boyfriend. I didn't know her ex-boyfriend that well, other than the normal small town stuff, but whatever happened resulted in a lot of closed door meetings with the partners and her. This is also the first case she's done more than research on since it happened.

"Dakota, you're the biggest badass lawyer we have. You've done all the research, you've prepped and talked to your client. The only thing that's left is to get into that court-room and kick some ass." I give her a smile that I hope reassures her, since I don't know the first thing about actually being in a courtroom.

Being the receptionist and office manager for Hammond Law in my hometown of Whiskey Falls wasn't where I thought I would be at thirty, but it's where I am, and I love it. The people here have been amazing, and very understanding about needing to take time off to care for Mom. It's been even better since Dakota joined, because now I also have a friend. Working full time and taking care of Mom doesn't leave a lot of free time to make friends and go out with people my age. Most of my interactions are with doctors, nurses, or clients.

It also doesn't leave any time for dating.

I miss dating.

Correction, I miss dating one person, but I can't think about him right now.

"Thank you, Ella." She opens her eyes as she drops her hand. "I need a distraction. What's going on with you?"

"You know nothing's going on with me. I go from here, to home, and back again."

"What about Derek?" The corner of Dakota's mouth ticked up into a smirk.

"Derek? The owner of The Book Barrel?"

"Yes, the owner of The Book Barrel! I've seen you two talk over books. I know he's even given you recommendations on romance novels before. He's totally into you."

"No, there's no way. We've known each other since we were babies! We went to school together. I knew him through his awkward teen years."

Sure, Derek is cute with his dark hair that falls just slightly over his eye and his black rimmed glasses that make him look intelligent and sophisticated. Not at all like the book nerd he was always called in school. But we were friends, and not the kind of friends that could turn into our own 'friends-to-lovers' trope. Strictly friends.

"He owns a bookstore, Dakota. Of course he's going to give me book recommendations."

"And he just happens to be into alien smut?" Her smirk grows wider as she steeples her fingers in front of her face.

I can see why people are intimidated by her in the court-room. She looks like she's about to interrogate me right now.

"And how would you know *that*?"

"Your love for alien smut?" Dakota laughs. "Don't worry, your secret is safe with me. I heard you and Derek discussing it when I was browsing the true crime books."

"Of course you were." I huff under her breath.

"What I really want to know is, why aliens? I'm genuinely curious."

I take a moment, trying to think of how to answer this without sounding like someone that's been heartbroken for the last ten years.

"I don't know. I'm tired of human men, I guess? The aliens seem to be obsessed with finding their true mate and doing everything they can to keep them."

"This wouldn't have to do with a certain country star from Whiskey Falls, would it?"

"Why would you think that?" I ask, straightening out my skirt that doesn't need to be straightened out. I uncross my legs and cross them again at my ankles, knowing I'm fidgeting more than I should.

"Lucky guess?" Dakota lets out a breath and leans forward in the chair. "It's okay to date, you know? I mean, he's…"

"Moved on? Attached to his long time girlfriend where they share an eight-year-old child? Obviously forgotten about me when I can't forget about him?" I'm rambling now. I know I am, but I can't help it. I haven't had anyone to talk about Greyson Wallace with in ten years, and now that I do, it seems to just be pouring out of me.

"Ella…"

"Don't. Please." I know the tone in her voice. It's the same tone I haven't been able to stand for ten years since he rolled out of town. If I hear that tone from Dakota I'm likely to start crying in her office, which is the last thing I want to happen.

She looks at me for another moment before sighing. "Fine. I still think you should make a go of it with Derek. You never know, it might surprise you."

"And what about you? Are you ready to jump into the dating field again after Laughlin?" I can't help but quip back, feeling defensive after her comment about a certain singer that's been banned from all conversation and thoughts.

"That's a little different."

"Maybe, but the thought is the same." I stand and turn to the door. I only make it two steps before I turn back around. "I don't know what happened with him, but I'm sorry. You deserve the best, Dakota."

"So do you, Ella." She gives me a kind, but sad, smile as she picks up the file folder she'd been looking for. "And thanks for this. I mean it, I don't know what I'd do without you."

I nod and make my way out of the office, afraid to speak. Emotions I'm not ready to deal with are lodged in my throat and if I let them up, I'll crumble.

Sitting back at my desk I tidy up the pens and papers, although nothing is out of place. I wiggle my mouse, waking my screen back up and look at the document I was working on before helping Dakota. I stare mindlessly at it, not really seeing what was in front of me.

I've worked so hard to push Greyson out of my mind. Most days I'm too busy with work or my mom to let thoughts of him creep in. I've mostly managed to avoid the country radio stations or talk of our hometown hero around town. Most people from Whiskey Falls know our tragic story and have the decency not to bring him up to me. Not that I blame Dakota. She wasn't here when my world fell apart. She didn't see how I was a twenty-year-old girl with heartbreak and too much responsibility to shoulder on my own.

She didn't see me lose my whole world, only to have to experience him moving on without me in the tabloids.

The screen on my phone lights up, alerting me to a text.

KRISSY

Brett's working late at the pub tonight. Come and keep me company?

I run through my usual excuses in my mind. I can't, I have too much work to do. My mom needs me. I have to get up early tomorrow, but for once, I don't want to. I want to go out and feel what it's like to be young and carefree. I don't get many nights where I can go out and do that.

Kody and Colton are back home now that the rodeo circuit is over for the season. They can sit with mom while I go out. One late weeknight out won't hurt.

I smile, picking up my phone and frantically type.

> I'd love to. What time?

What? Really? No begging? No coercing? What gives?

Don't change your mind. Meet me at the Lucky Dog at 7.

> You want me to sit with you in your fiancé's bar so you can stare at him all night, don't you? Lol. And maybe I just decided I need a night out. Don't make me regret it.

I would never.

And you can't blame me wanting to stare at him. He's hot.

I laugh as I slide my phone into my desk drawer. Leave it to Krissy to want a night with a friend but keep her fiancé close by. They've been inseparable since they got together and getting engaged has only made it worse. As much as I'm happy for her, it also makes me sad. I thought I'd have that. I thought Greyson and I would be married and have a couple of kids by now. He would be out singing or working on the ranch while I stayed at home chasing mini-Greyson's around.

But it wasn't meant to be.

Instead, my dad passed away, leaving my mom with no one to care for her after her MS diagnosis. Her health rapidly declined after that. She seemed to have lost the will to fight after losing the love of her life. I can't say I blame her, but that doesn't make any of it any easier.

My gaze falls on the framed picture I have of me, my brothers, and my mom last summer, laughing by the lake, everyone looking so happy. Everyone but my mom. I can see the smile doesn't reach her eyes, and it hasn't for twelve years. I look at me in the picture, my face turned to Colton so I can't see my eyes. I wonder if the same can be said for me. Greyson might not have died, but the hope and the future I'd planned for us did. It hurt so much more when I found out the rumours were true and he'd gotten some woman pregnant a few years after he left Whiskey Falls, only to have stayed with her since then. I remember how the town seemed unable to look me in the eye or only speak to me in hushed tones for months, almost afraid to be the ones to break the news to me.

But I knew, and it hurt worse than I ever could have imagined.

Wiping a tear from my eye I straighten my spine, deciding here and now I won't be that woman anymore. I may not have tried for love for the past ten years, but I'm ready to let my love for Greyson stay where it belongs. In the past.

Taking my phone out of my drawer, I shoot another quick text to Krissy before I chicken out.

> I want to try something new. Meet me at my place at 6:30?

About the Author

Kimberly Ann lives in BC, Canada with her husband, two children and ridiculously cute German Shepherd. When she's not dreaming of stories, she homeschools her two children as they explore and learn the world together, reads anything she can get her hands on, and drinks a lot of coffee.

Growing up with her head lost in a book, it was no surprise when she picked up a pen, or her laptop, to write her own. Kimberly Ann's stories are based on the world around her as she brings her imagination to life with stories of small towns, swoon-worthy men, and the women that keep them on their toes.

Also by Kimberly Ann

To view other books by Kimberly Ann, please visit her website at
www.kimberlyannauthor.com

Manufactured by Amazon.ca
Bolton, ON

34789854R00048